GRETEL

ANNALEE ADAMS

GRETEL

First edition. October 2018.

Copyright © 2018 Annalee Adams.

The moral rights of the author have been asserted.

Written by Annalee Adams.

This is a work of fiction. Similarities to real people, places, or events are entirely coincidental.

ISBN 97817 308 992 70

This book has been typeset in Garamond.

www.AnnaleeAdams.biz

For Angel, May, and Jessica

All that we see or seem
Is but a dream within a dream.

Edgar Allen Poe

1

Warped by the mindset of a child's dream, I lay frigid and alone. Stripped of my childhood, naked and abandoned, awaiting my punishment.

I didn't mean to; my hand had slipped. I couldn't help but shake when he entered the room. He was the unknown, the tall cumbersome mass of an assailant, as he walked through the darkness of the underground tunnel, speaking in riddles to unseen ghosts and darkened spirits. He had lost his mind years ago, it was only her that kept him sane, that kept us alive.

I didn't believe he was totally human. When Jess went missing it was bad enough. Her tortured screams ripped through the tunnels, absorbed into the walls. If you listen close, put your ear to the moss-covered brickwork… you can hear her. Her wail is eternal, like the drumming beat of the pulse beneath your skin. Skin that is covered in grime, festering faeces under chapped fingernails, a cauldron of infection waiting to burst into boils and blisters. My hair so long it covered my breasts, clinging on with the grease of every day since the day he took me. Knotted like a bird's nest, it kept me warm and hid the bruises from the beatings over the years.

He said he'd saved us, brought us down from the cruel misgivings of the world above. He believed himself a saviour, a man chosen by God to free the souls of the children of the North. But we aren't children anymore, we are youths, teenagers aching to step into the world, witness the sunlight, believe in the promise of life and love. But no, he'd rather see us burn than allow us a glimpse of the life we once had.

All I had left of my old life was my pocket mirror. I looked down to see such a simple treasure. It had been a lifesaver over the years, it gave me the ability to see when our captor was coming. My body tensed as I recalled the first time I saw his face through the mirror, the first time I realized what my life would become. I'd been applying lip gloss on the corner of Anchorage Street, ready to cross the road and head home after a night out with friends. I was thirteen back then, new to the exotic world of boys, the rebellious lure of strangers and the promise of being home before dark. We'd stopped out late though, sunset had been and gone. I stood under the lamplight gazing in my mirror as the scarred face of a hooded man appeared behind me. That's when the night sky fled from my eyes, my body felt heavy and my head hit the ice-cold pavement. He preserved us, preserved our innocence by keeping us locked up for years.

I missed them, my family; they were all I had growing up. I had time to think, sitting here in this claustrophobic space. I was abandoned, sealed in a small cage, kept in by metal bars. I took a deep breath and sighed, my eyes welled with tears, my body trembled. I missed my mother, I missed her smile, her voice, the smell of the rose scented perfume when she held me close. My mother was an artist, a lover of life, inspired by the beauty in another's expression. I remember her sitting for hours at a café; me with a milkshake, her with a coffee, as she gazed at the reality around us. She said there was so much love out there in life, so much beauty all around us, she called life her inspiration, and I, her muse. I smiled, I wonder if she still looks out in hope at that coffee shop, if she prays for my safe return, or am I another runaway, another missing poster on the wall of Bancock station?

I held my knees up to my chest, lowered my head and wept through the darkness. What was he going to do with me now? I panted for air, crying harder than before. Gasping through the tightness of my chest, I choked on the tears as they fell. The taste of salt coated my tongue, bile retched up through my throat, only to be swallowed down again as I breathed rapidly, losing focus. My eyelids fluttered, pain enraged the back of my throat and I panicked myself into a pit of surreal desperation. Was this it? Was this the end? The day I die, a forgotten scream hidden within these walls. My head pounded, heavy and burdened. I needed my mom, my dad and those big bear cuddles he gave when I awoke scared by a nightmare.

My father was a big fellow, stocky and stern, but just and fair. He gave the most perfect cuddles any daughter could wish for. But at thirteen I didn't need them anymore before I was taken I was full of life, bright and free in the world of the living. My life changed when I hit my teenage years, rebellious and hanging around the local shopping mall with my friends. We'd snuck in to watch The Shining at Heedy's movie theatre. Totally freaked by Jacks killing spree, Sarah screamed and hid in her seat… that's when old John Heedy found us and chased us around the theatre, threatening to phone our parents. We talked him out of it though, afraid of what our moms would say about our new rebellious nature. I never did get to see the end of that film. I should have let Mr. Heedy ring my mom if I had… I might have seen her again. But now five years later, and I'm still here, stinking in this dump. Still alive, still sane, and now very much alone.

2

Over the years girls had come and gone, one at a time they'd arrive, but none would last. Jess had always been there though, she was the sister I'd never had, the friend I'd always keep. I made it through every day because she kept me going. She'd sit in the corner brushing my tangled hair, plaiting each strand into an elegant style. We didn't have any bands, so we'd rip apart our old clothes, they were too small for us anyway, but they made the perfect fabric ties. We loved to giggle about it, posing in my cracked pocket mirror, using the dirt on the floor for eyeshadow. That was until my first Christmas there in the cage. We knew it was Christmas time as our hefty captor always brought in an old brown tree with a few broken lights attached to it. It was something to look forward to, and that first Christmas when he gave us a white nightgown each, we felt like princesses dressed for a ball. With elegant hair, exquisite eyeshadow and sparkling new dresses, we were the catch of the century, like Cinderella escaping to meet her prince by the light of her fairy godmother. He must have liked our performance as he updated his camera system, watching from afar. Next came Halloween, pumpkins carved into scary faces, candles flickering within. Our treat would be a candy bar which we savoured and relished, delighting in the fairytale of Hansel and Gretel as we performed the show to the camera, our captor the witch in this nightmarish tale. If we broke the chocolate right it'd last for days, melting in our mouths like glorious heaven, or the sunrise on the beach of Olden Bay.

I remember when Nancy arrived, screaming and crying for her mummy. There was little Jess, or I could do, we tried talking to her, easing her pain. Bringing life back into her sunken eyes with our dancing and dramatic shows that we'd created. But nothing would warm the sorrowful expression she gave. She was too far gone, we couldn't save her in time. He said she wasn't worth preserving, the light had gone from her eyes, the world had gotten to her already. She was the first of many new souls, one every six months or so. Each taken too late, each soul destroyed by the reality above us. That's when they screamed, kicking and pleading as he took them, dragging them from our cage, fingernails broke in the dirt, tears soiled the floor as they left us. Jess would hold me tight, bury my head in her chest. I couldn't bear the tears, the torment. The sound of cracking bones and the wail of terror as their fleeting lives were taken from them. It lasted too long, each child shattered by their sins, freed from their life so they could dance once again in Heaven. But when their silence came, we knew it was over. The walls grew quiet again and the children of the night were forgotten.

Jess said we were lucky, she protected me, he preserved me. We were both alive because we willed it so. Jess had taken me under her wing, loved me like a sister should. She took the beatings for me when he became angry, she pleaded my purpose in the world. I'd only survived as long as I had because she had my back. It wasn't Jess's fault though, my caged roommate grew to love him, she said it was hard not to over the years. She had been here over ten years, taken as an eight-year-old. She looked up to him, even welcomed the beatings, she said his touch made her feel alive again. I'd only lasted five years so far, how she carried on for so long before me I'll never know. I guess when there's no-one else to talk to, no-one to see, then even the beatings of an insane madman made you feel alive.

It wasn't right though, Jess never got to see the light of day again. Maybe I won't either, maybe I'll stay here until I wither and age, become a stale pile of urine mushed up as my body dwindles, dying in a rotted mess in the corner. After she'd gone the cage felt bare, the light she brought had diminished and nothing but darkness took her place. I slept for days wrapped in the green woollen blanket we'd been given for our second Christmas together. We'd shared it every time we slept, snuggled together for warmth, sleeping our childhood away. The tattered old thing brought us comfort, gave us hope, something to look forward to. Every morning we awoke in darkness, he'd arrive with a bucket of sloppy porridge for breakfast. Jess arose and marked off the calendar he'd given us last New Year's Day. We counted the days, the months and the years like this, that's how we knew how long we'd survived his capture. I'd like to say knowing what day it was brought me hope. It did for Jess, but for me… it meant another day I'd been forgotten, my parents moved on, my friends moved away. After the first couple of years it became easier, we planned shows, concentrated on creating a life in the cage for ourselves. But I always missed home, no matter how much we danced it would never be the same as dancing around my bedroom singing in the hairbrush to Madonna. I miss the days of sleepovers and pillow fights. I'd lost too much.

After she was gone, I was alone for months in our cage, forgotten, erased from time. He rarely passed by, only to throw in a bucket of scraps to eat every now and then. I lost the track of the days, there was no routine anymore. I couldn't tell if it was morning or night, everything was turned upside down. I wondered if he'd abandoned all hope, leaving me alone to wither and die. The thought petrified me, my skin crawled with the fear of dying a death alone. But then the despair of his sickening touch, the stench of his musty smoke-filled clothing. I gagged at the memory of it. If she was no longer here, then what hope did I have any more?

I'd surrendered my life to the elements, all dreams diminished… that's when the new girls arrived. One by one they came, taken from their slumber. It'd become quite the crowd, as three more joined me. The first girl arrived in a filthy nightie with a picture of a pink bear on. The bear had a white tummy with a colourful rainbow. She said he was her best friend and then proceeded to show me her replica teddy bear that he'd bought in with her. Her face was dirtied by chocolate as he'd lured her in with the promise of sugared candy and soda pops. This little girls name was Beth, she said she lived at 22 Nightingale street and wanted to go home. She sat softly crying in the corner cuddling her bear. I wrapped her in the blanket and soothed her tears, just as Jess once had for me. At the young age of four, she was new to the world above, she sat frightened holding me tight. I knew he'd be happy with her progress, she was young, pliable and easy to manipulate. Her soft brown curls cradled her tiny face as I wiped the tears away and she fell sound asleep in my arms.

Susie was the second girl with long blond hair and a bright smile. She must have been about fourteen and seemed besotted by him. Perhaps he'd wooed her, promised her the Earth as she naively skipped along beside him. She sat for days smiling at the camera auditioning for her part, completely unaware of the tragedy of the situation she found herself in. With Susie came a Walkman, a set of headphones and her favourite mix tape. She delighted at introducing me to the hit songs by Cyndi Lauper, Madonna, and Tina Turner. We danced for hours until her battery finally gave out.

The final girl was called Leah, with short brown hair and a rugged attitude. She wasn't his normal type, this one was a tomboy with every ounce of fight still left in her. She wouldn't last long in here. She spent days scurrying along the walls screaming for a way out. She was a manic twelve-year-old with a love of baseball, hockey, and dogs. I often thought that maybe he really had saved her from whatever messed up upbringing she'd come from. Leah arrived with a baseball cap that had two baseball cards tucked in the side. She called them her all-time favourite players. One was Rickey Henderson, who she said played at Dodger Stadium in 1980 when her Dad took her to her first ever game. The other was Mike Schmidt, who in 1982 was one of the top twelve players at the Veterans Park, he was her new idol after her Dad left and her mum turned to drink.

Now there were more of us, our captor came down every day and the routine of sloppy porridge started off the mornings again. He fitted a bulb to the roof of the tunnel, leading wiring back to an old generator far from sight. If it weren't for the constant buzzing, I'd have enjoyed the new light source. But it kept me awake at night, my eyes bled with dark purple circles underneath. I was tired, worn down and needed sleep.

The next morning when he arose, he threw in a new calendar with the days crossed off up-to-date. He wanted to start again, a fresh new cycle, a new beginning. He limped across the ground, holding two pumpkins. They'd been carved with the face of a bloodthirsty killer, jaws wide, teeth sharpened, backlit by a candle flickering within. It was Halloween again; another year had passed by. I knew it meant the salivating candy, the trick or treat, the fun, and the games. But this time it was different. Jess's upbeat attitude had disappeared from my life, and no matter how hard I forced myself forward I couldn't enjoy this Halloween without her.

When he bought the chocolate, the girls tore it apart, each wanting a taste. I lay on the blanket, cold and alone, watching from afar as they ate the bar without consent. They were happy though, smiling for the first time in a long time, even Leah had calmed down. I was just too tired to reach out and take some. Beth broke a piece off, ran over to me and sat snuggled in the blanket offering me some. I took it gratefully, smiled and suckled the chocolate until it was all gone. She slept beside me that night, waking only to the horror of the cage we were kept in. Her tears were soothed by the fairytales I spoke of. It reminded me of the show Jess and I had put on. She had played Gretel, I became Hansel; trapped and caged up ready to be eaten by the evil witch. Gretel always saved me though, always protected me from the torment. Beth enjoyed the stories, the fact that no matter how hideous life seemed, there was always a Gretel that could take the pain away.

That's when he came, unlocked the huge cage door and ordered me to stand, assist him in his morning duties. Jess used to do this, she used to be the one that left and helped him prepare the food for the day. It was my turn now, I'd taken her place and had to mother the children within my care. This was it, the turning point in my life, the chance to create something better, to seek out a plan of action, to push forward and reach freedom. Was it possible? Could there ever be a way out of this nightmare? I'd hoped so, but then my tired shaking hands spilt the tea.

When the tea hit the floor I froze, my porcelain face panicked, my mouth agape. He was coming, and I'd be punished for this insolence. He slapped my face, as heat bled through pain, causing me to gasp, shriek out in anguish. I shouldn't have though, he disliked the noise, we were to only speak when spoken to. By crying out

I'd made things worse. He gripped my arm tight and threw me in the smaller cage, the place where punishment became reality. Gritting his teeth, he locked the steel bars, leaving the key in sight but far from reach. The icy concrete chilled through me as salty tears cushioned my lips. Was this it? Was this the end? Trapped in dismay, I shuddered, there must be a way out. I'd searched for so long, dreaming of one day getting back to my mom and dad. I'd always been a daddy's girl, loved the bear hugs as he tucked me in at night. He was my hero. As for mum, I always enjoyed her magical bedtime stories as a child… and those shoes, the bright yellow heels I wore with my fluorescent socks and shell suit. I can remember dancing around the apartment, mom terrified I'd break my neck. We didn't have much, but we had each other. Were they still searching for me? With missing posters splashed across the town, did my face make it onto an old milk carton, thrown in the bin like a memory forgotten and discarded?

Maybe this was how my life would end, nearly eighteen and trapped for the last five years. I'd been alone for hours after he killed Jess, days even. I remember how his coat was covered in blood. He leaped from the room screeching, saying she made him do it. Bloodied fists pummelled the walls. I'd never before heard him raise his voice in such a way. It was the noise of the chainsaw and the bloody footprints that gave him away. He shifted binbags from one room to another, blood dribbled from the safety hole at the bottom of the bag. Would I be next? Did my future look as tragic as hers had? Was my body about to be cut up and laid out? Tossed aside like a ragdoll thrown from a cradle.

I looked around, hardly able to move for the lack of space I was confined in. My body ached, I needed to stretch, but my arms wouldn't fit through the gaps between the bars. This cage was smaller, a lot smaller. It was meant for the capture of an animal, the transportation of a dog perhaps, not the punishment of a teenage girl. It was cold, damp and smelt of burning flesh. That seared overcooked roast of a human that once took the name of Jess. He'd been playing with fire, I feared the reason why. Had he lit the oven? Prepared the stove? I shuddered at the thought of the old fairytale creeping back into my mind. My Gretel had gone, cooked and eaten by the evil witch. The stench was revolting, surrounding my skin like a straitjacket, unable to release myself from the putrid torture he put me through. How long would I be here? Would I ever see the girls again? I promised Beth that one day we'd be free. She called me her Gretel, her protector, and her friend. Would I survive this Halloween night intact, or would I be removed from their lives in bin bags, my blood dripping to the floor as I'm dumped in the garbage outside?

For saying five years had passed it was hard to conceive what I looked like. I knew I had aged over the years; my pocket mirror had shown me that. But the small space of reality it portrayed, never gave me the whole picture of my body, my heart, or my soul. I wasn't just a child anymore, I was growing into a woman. My body bled every month, my breasts matured, hair grew where it should never be seen. Jess said I was becoming a woman like she had when she died. My nightdress that once covered me like a tent, now defined my shape, gave birth to my curves and barely covered my bottom with its tattered edging. My dirty blonde hair touched the floor where I sat, grating at my body with its matte texture. My baby blue eyes had suffered in silence over the years, having seen too much, cried for too long, their sparkle had died by Jess's side when all hope was lost, and I found myself trapped in another cage again.

How long had I been trapped within this tiny secluded cage? My stomach rumbled, my eyes threatened to close. I was beyond tired, past reasoning with reality as I closed my eyes and prayed I'd wake from this nightmare. Is it even day or night down here? Did the World still exist out there? According to Leah, it's pretty much the same as I remember it but with less Madonna and more Metallica, whoever that was.

I wondered if my parents would still recognize me. What about Joe on the seventh floor. Did he hold out hope? We were dating Joe and me. I remember holding hands by the swings, with the safety of a cuddle or the love of our first kiss. He was mine and I was his. We'd grown up together, I remember marrying him at the sweet age of eight. Nothing could tear us apart, we were meant to be, the type of childhood sweethearts written about in love stories and romantic comedies. He was funny, always made me laugh, I wish I could hear his laughter one more time. But in the darkness of the cage, there's no place for laughter, no faint shadow of life left within these walls. I'd stopped crying, falling into the depressive state of nothingness, knowing that this

Halloween, this night, it may be my last. I feared what he'd do to me, but crying wouldn't help, he'd enjoy the screams, knowing he'd released another of the world's demons back down into Hell. Why did he see us as these creatures? Why did he believe we were darker than the nightmare we lived in? We were only children, taken too young. Ripped from our mothers' bosom as she cried alone in the night.

3

Huddled up I opened my eyes, the time had passed without recollection, minutes into hours, hours into days. How long had I been here? What's the point anymore, why keep fighting? It's just another day of darkness, another day of cowering in the corner. Jess had always opted to be chosen, she seemed to enjoy his company after a while. Her need for his attention was what got her killed in the end. I missed her so damn much, she was the big sister I'd never had, my only family in this hell hole of an existence. She'd protected me all these years. Surely, it's my turn to take the heat and protect the new girls. That's fair, it's right really. So why do my knees tremble at the thought of him touching me? I know it'll happen eventually, he's tried before, but Jess pleaded for him to take her instead. It's better me than one of the new girls, they're too young, too innocent, they don't know what it's like living down here. Leah won't last long, not if she keeps pushing him like that, he'll make an example out of her, and then there'll be bin bags and chainsaws all over again.

I wish I knew what the time was, not that it really made a difference. But if I knew the time I'd have some idea of when he'd be back. Jess and I would count the number of minutes he'd take after he bought breakfast, to when he'd collect her for her morning chores. Time would be a luxury right now. I know he's watching me, seeing if he can make me squirm, there are cameras all over these tunnels. I shuddered with the cold, a bristling wind crept through the tunnel. That was strange though, I hadn't felt the movement of wind caressing my body for what seemed like a lifetime. If there was wind, there was a way it got in. If there was a way in, then there was a way out. There had to be? Jess had played along with my fantasies of freedom over the years, she'd laughed at my hopeless attempts to dig my way out of the tunnel. A plastic spoon didn't last so long on the dark damp concrete or the grey brick wall. But this wasn't one of those times. I'd actually felt a chill, shivered from a touch of an unseen force. Perhaps it was Jess, perhaps the shriek of her spirit wasn't the only thing entrapped in these walls. Perhaps her soul still wandered, looking for a way out.

My body trembled, hairs stood on end. The cool air resurfaced and the darkness began to ease. The softened hue of a flickering light crept into the room. The cage I sat in was at the side of the room, a hidey-hole in the tunnel away from prying eyes. Around me, the darkness waned. A silhouette of light cast its shadows over a stack of old crates on the far side. Shapes formed, and I could see the remains of broken plates littering the floor. Something had happened here. I held my breath, uncertain of where I was. Gasping for air, I shivered. Tell me this isn't where he killed her? I gulped. My body tensed, fists balled as my broken nails plunged into the palms of my hands. Tears welled in my eyes, falling one by one. They cushioned my dry lips as I absorbed their salty exterior. My nerves erupted, body trembled, and I gripped the side of the cage, shaking it, screaming to be let free. She had died here. I was certain of it. My heart wrenched, sobbing at the reality of the nightmare I lived in, broken down by the forced nature of my insignificant life. I was trapped, and there was only one reason I was trapped in this room. He was going to kill me, and no fairytale could save me this time.

My body felt so weak from the lack of sleep, I'd hardly eaten or drank anything in days. He wanted me weak, he wanted me pliable. What fight could I put up against a beast like him? I sobbed, my throat burned from the choking sensation of my cries. My arms ached from trying to break apart the bars, pushing and pulling until my breath gave way in my lungs. I panted, gasping for life, gripping it with both hands. I couldn't let him do this to me. This couldn't be it. This couldn't be all I lived for.

A bright circular light streamed across the wall, bouncing as he walked, growing bigger, brighter with every step he took. He was coming, this was it. I crawled into the corner of the cage. Braced me, making myself as small as I could. Gripping my knees, I buried my head in my hands, tensed up ready for the final blow.

The sound of heavy footsteps drummed through me. Thud. Thud. Thud, then silence. He was there, stood towering above my cage. I didn't need to look to fear his presence. The smell of sweat and old cigarettes engulfed the air, causing me to gag, repulsed by his odour. I lifted head, broke open my eyelids and his colossal appearance came into view. His bulky body was wrapped in aged clothes; a checked shirt with a musty stench and an old blood stain. Baggy trousers gave his spindle like legs coverage, stretched over his hefty gut as he pulled on his belt strap, his keys jangling to tease me.

He bent down, reached through the cage with his grimy hand. His touch made me recoil, shrinking into the bars, trying to get away from him. He caressed the bare skin on my leg, hushed back my tears, but it only made me cry harder.

"Now don't worry Lucy," he said. "I know it was an accident."

The bulky body of a fifty-year-old man stood up, pulled away and limped across the abandoned room. Lighting candles on top of a crate, he glared at the remains of something besides him. He appeared to mumble, complain and gesture with both fists. He was arguing as he sat on another crate, straightening the makeshift table that held the elegant candlesticks before him.

"Shush now Jess!" he yelled, "I'll tell her." He leaned forward to the other side of the table and caressed something across from him. What was it?

"Jess wants you to know she's missed you." He scowled, looking over at my frail figure trapped in a cage. My throat hurt as I held back the scream of dampened tears. I'd cried so hard for so long, it physically hurt to cry any longer. He was more insane than I'd thought, he'd well and truly lost any sanity he had left. Jess was dead, he'd killed her; chopped her up into little pieces and threw her out with the trash. Didn't he? Then why was he talking to her as though she was sat beside him?

Around him, the floor gleamed red, old blood stains had sunk into the concrete, lit by the candlelight that wavered around him. He kept his torch turned on, placed it on the table and directed its glare. It shone across the room, giving life to its surroundings, dust particles drifted across the light, as darkness dwindled away. Its stern glare directed its energy on one particular spot, something dark, bony and crawling with creatures. The remains of a previous owner's torso sat upright on the side wall, rotted and skeletal, it fed the rats as they came out to play. I gasped, my hand rushed to my mouth. It couldn't be Jess, could it? No, she'd only been gone for hours… days even? I couldn't tell, how could I tell? It was too far gone, the remains of flesh eaten away by the carnivorous rats that infested this graveyard. Was it one of my old roommates? One of the girls he'd taken, perhaps Nancy or Sarah? Both had succumbed to the slash of his blade. How many victims came before me? How many souls had he destroyed? Did he clean out the cage like the witch did, welcoming Hansel and Gretel in, fattening them up for supper? Why keep it there though? Didn't he care? Was it a scare tactic, a way of saying 'this could be you?'

On the top of the crate where the candles stood, he placed two broken plates, piecing them back together to form some sort of dining area. Plastic knives and forks were arranged neatly, and a large carving knife was placed in the centre of the table. Standing up he trudged over to the right side of the room, picked up the carcass of a chicken and slammed it back on its broken platter. Grumbling about something under his breath, he limped back over to the table with it. The dead roast established its place in the centre of the crate, beside the lambent light of the cream coloured candles. I searched the room, panicking, screaming out inside for a means of escape, yet no words came out. His presence had me at a disadvantage. I wasn't ready for what he planned next. I wouldn't ever be ready for the final moments, but it was coming, he was preparing, and the thing beside him agreed. Every so often the flicker of the two candles warmed the face of the thing that sat beside him. It wasn't the shape of a person, nor the shape of any creature I knew. But whatever he spoke to, never spoke back. Did it live? Did it ever live?

The wall behind it was lit by the candles. Any wall usually enveloped an unnerving desire of freedom within me, but instead, this wall gave way to a splattering of a recent bloodbath. Jess. The floor shone with the remains of a fallen body. My skin crawled as I gulped back the bile that formed in my throat. What was it he was talking to? I couldn't quite make it out. It looked handmade, handstitched almost. Covered in blood, a carcass of a former being. Nausea hit again. Tears began to fall. Who was it? I knew the answer. I just couldn't say. Couldn't allow me to take in the severity of the situation. Was that really Jess sat there?

My stomach tightened, I swallowed back the saliva again and again. Was this really happening?

My throat clenched, body shivered. I couldn't stop it. My mind swirled. Body retched, and out came the chocolate, the last meal I'd eaten. My throat burned, stomach bruised. He stood up, turned towards me and glared. I held my breath, gripped my knees and braced my body in a cocoon, fearful of what would happen next.

"Come here Lucy," he demanded, shuffling his way towards the cage door.

"No, no I'm fine here," I stuttered.

"Come and sit with us for dinner, Lucy. Jess has spent a long time cooking."

I dug my heels into the floor, held on to the bars. I wasn't going anywhere. His keychain jangled as he pulled out a large silver key, unlocked the cage door and yanked it open. The sound of metal being dragged over the concrete echoed across the room. He scowled down at me, his wiry beard tinged with grey hairs that shrouded half of his face. It'd grown so much in the last few years.

When he'd stole me from the night, he'd appeared younger, fresher, stronger even. Granted he still had a limp. Jess said it was from shrapnel in the Falklands war. But even with his limp he always found a way to outrun me. After my sixth escape attempt, he punished me in a new way. I didn't receive the usual beatings or broken bones. Instead, I was made to do something so horrendous that I never tried to escape again. He hadn't hurt me or Jess. But he did make me bow down, take the knife and call over our beloved pet dog, Max. He watched, glaring at me, willing me to take the dog's life. Jess pleaded forgiveness, begged him to leave Max alone. But he wouldn't. Max was our friend. Our captor had given him to us on the fourth Christmas I'd spent locked up there. Jess adored him, we both did. He was a fluffy little cocker spaniel full of life and love, always ready to curl up beside us, lick our wounds and join in dancing when we made up another show. I couldn't do it.

I'd never hurt anyone before. I dropped the knife in protest. But he picked it up, held it to Jess's neck, told me it was her or the dog. I made a choice. One I had to live with. I don't think she ever forgave me for killing him.

That's when things changed between Jess and me, she became more distant with me, craving his attention instead. She'd sit there staring at the camera, plaiting her hair, and singing made up songs, enticing him over to her. That's when the two of them began to fall for one another. He paid no interest in me anymore, for that I was thankful. Instead, he was all over her. I'd often hear her laughing as he'd pulled her from our cell. It wasn't strange for her to be gone for hours, as laughter filled the shallow tunnels and the two of them danced before candlelight.

My mind snapped back to reality as his clammy hand reached in, grabbed my ankle with and yanked me out of the cage. I screamed, held on for dear life, kicking out in protest. He slapped at my feet, grabbed both ankles and continued to pull me free from the cage.

"Lucy!" he yelled. "Let go!"

I cried, wailed in fact. I couldn't let him take me, this cage provided the safety I needed, it kept me hidden away, safe and sound. I needed to stay here, afraid of what he'd do if I let go.

He stood up, pulled my ankles high up into the air. He was too strong, I couldn't hold on for much longer. My body was being stretched, pulled through the vice-like grip of the rack. His foot braced against the cage as he wrenched me backward. Pain pulsed through me as my grip extended to my fingertips, then to my nails, as he ripped me backward out of the cage, hitting the floor, knocking me unconscious.

4

When I came to, my eyes opened, flickering between light and dark. My head felt heavy, throbbed with every blink of my eyelids. The drumming beat made me wince as the light scoured out my eyes. I brought my right hand to my face, reached up to my forehead, but it felt strange, numb almost as if some barrier was in place between me and my body.

"You're awake," he said, with an upward twinge of the lips.

"What?" I questioned, silently yelping at the pain when I spoke. My hand reached my lips as the searing pain of something taught pulled at me. "What is it?" I asked, trying as little as possible to move my mouth. Something was on my face, covering me like a barbed blanket. The taste of iron rimmed across my mouth as I gulped back blood, aware my lips weren't working as well as they should be.

Feeling around my face I found tufts of hair that weren't my own, mashed up with knots of string, that when I pulled I yelped. My eyes stretched out through a tunnel, looking through the covering of something cold and tough around them. What had he done to me?

"You look beautiful," he said, offering me my broken pocket mirror. I thought I'd never see it again, I thought he'd thrown it in the trash like he had with Jess's body. I leaned forward to take it, noticing I was sat at the table with the fractured plates and disposable cutlery. Looking down I saw I'd been dressed like a broken doll in a floral outfit, something hideous and old-fashioned that my grandmother would have worn. Taking the mirror from his thick grimy hand, I saw that as I gripped the outside of the clasp, my cracked nails were painted red to match the roses adorning the dress I wore. Unclicking it I opened the mirror, brought it to my face and stared blindly in horror.

The face above my own was not one of my making. It was the rotting remains of Jess's former body, her nose held mine in place, her cheeks dug into my own, eye sockets encircled my retinas and rosy red lips were fastened over me like a mask. He'd used thick black thread to stitch me in place, sewn into my flesh while I lay unconscious and vulnerable. He'd taken my body, changed it into hers, and I'd disappeared beneath it.

"You'll be wanting this Jess," he said, passing me a ruby red lipstick. "It's your favourite colour, just like Mama's," he said, looking pleased.

Silence. That's all I could do. Sit quietly like a lamb ready for slaughter. Silence.

"What's wrong?" he asked, his forehead crumpled into a frown. "Put on the lipstick," he demanded slamming his fist on the table. I jumped, picked up the lipstick and drew over her lips, shaking and making a mess of the lipstick. He leaned over, his lips slanted upwards as he reached in his pocket for a dirty tissue, wiping the smudge from our face. The tissue was stained red when he pulled away, a mix of lipstick and blood from my ever-peeling face. I gagged without him noticing.

"There, much better, don't you think?" he asked, pushing my hand upwards so the mirror I gripped showed my face.

I whimpered.

"Don't you think!"

I nodded, crying softly as her skin protected my tears and hid them from his glare.

I was overwhelmed, hit by a state of shock, fight and flight banished me to a frozen puddle of mess and I couldn't do anything. Who was I now? My face screamed at the sharpness of every movement I made. The slightest glance to the side pulled at my strings as my puppet master held me close by. I tried to look around, search for any means of escape. I wanted her face pulled off me, no matter the searing pain or anguish. I had to know I was still alive under there. That I too wasn't cut up, faceless and sewn onto another of the girls. Would I know? Would I feel if my face no longer existed?

Looking to the right, a wall of crates stood five high, stacked on top of each other like a Jenga puzzle threatening to give way. The chill of the concrete floor shuddered through me, my bare feet blue from the cold, cyanosed as my circulation failed within. I should be used to the bare nature of my entrapment by now, but when you live in fear, everything's uncertain.

Looking up I bumped into his scabbed hand as he reached forward. I stopped like a deer in headlights, motionless, frozen to the core. His hand touched me, and I played dead. He brushed against our face, reaching further forward, brushing my hair, untangling the knots.

Turning around to face the table, the candlelight shimmered across the thing next to me. I hadn't noticed it was sat so close, what was it? As he took his hand away I looked to the left, repulsed by his touch. The thing beside me was covered in blood. I gulped, retching saliva in my throat as I took in the ghastly sight before my eyes. The stench of necrotic flesh was almost unbearable. The remains of a head sat upright on top of a mannequin, the face had been carved off, as bloody muscles covered its cheekbones. Remains of tissue had been fastened to the plastic body, giving a resemblance to Jess, his former loved one. Looking closer, squinting a little, I saw a pair of familiar eyes staring back at me. I yelped. It couldn't be, could it? Bloodied skin threaded its way across the face. This was the head of a friend I once knew, a sister I'd always loved, she was my protector, my Gretel, and he'd chopped her up, redesigning her body to suit his own morbid fantasies.

"Aren't you going to say hello to Lucy, Jess?"

I bounded backward, the static pitch of my continuous scream ricocheted through the room. The crate under me flipped forward as I backed off, toppling into the wall of crates and knocking the remains of Jess over. Her football head lopsided, falling off the mannequin, bouncing across the cold concrete floor.

"Jess!" he yelled as my scream continued, fists balled up, back tense and legs shaking. I cowered in the darkest corner I could find. I couldn't see her remains, couldn't stare into those glacial eyes again. He ran over to retrieve the skinned head of Jess and place it back on the grubby mannequin.

"Jess," he yelled. "That's not very nice," he shouted, directing his glare at me. He thought I was Jess, saw the dead head that rolled on the floor as my own. He limped over, grabbed me by my hair and dragged my shaken body across the floor. "Say sorry to Lucy!" he yelled as he pushed me down beside the mannequin, shoving my face into her head. "SAY SORRY!" I was face to face with the head of my former best friend. She was dead, cold, slaughtered and skinned as her bruised skin dressed the mannequin, like an overcoat caresses its owner.

"Say sorry, damn it!" he yelled, slapping me across the side of my head.

I cried I couldn't do it anymore, this was it, this was my end and there was no escaping it. I'd be the next mannequin at the tea party as he spoke for me, ready to play with the next girl, or the next, or the one after that. How long would I stay fresh? How long until I started to smell, skin rotting, unpreserved and blackened, just as she was.

He pushed me to the ground. Kicked me in the ribs. I choked. Tears filled my eyes as everything around me blurred. Holding my head down onto the slimy floor he yelled, "you've upset her now." He kicked me again, I coughed through her lips and blood shot out before me. My body trembled as I lay frozen on the ground, his enormous figure rose above me. "She's dead damn you," he screamed. "You killed her." Blunt force trauma impacted my ribs again, and I cradled myself from his beatings, cocooned in tears as my body spasmed, and I screamed, crying through the pain.

"She looked up to you, how could you?" Was he crying now too? His stifled breath edged across me as he knelt sobbing into my broken body. "Why did you do this Jess, why?" he asked. Tears soaked into my dress as I cried harder, deeper. "She loved you, we both did, I never asked you to kill her." He wiped the tears from his grubby face as I lay shaking, trembling, pained by broken ribs, distraught from the face sewn onto my own but relieved as I knew this would all end soon. Clambering on top of me he forced my arms away from my head. I gave in, given up on the fight, ready to die by his hand and be at peace once and for all. "Open your eyes," he yelled. "Face her, face what you did."

"I didn't," I whispered, shaking my head. I knew it'd anger him, I didn't care anymore. I didn't kill her, would never kill my best friend. I grieved through my tears, panting for breath, panicked through the sobs of a broken child.

"WHAT!" he screamed, "What did you say?" He yanked my hair back, exposed my neck and squeezed tight. Both hands gripped harder as I shook and spasmed. This was it, this was the end, relief rushed through my body as I gave in to the unjust pain, welcoming death just as it nearly came. Letting go before my consciousness slipped away, he stroked my hair, smelled the dirt within it. His moist breath wet my earlobes, "Mama said

I couldn't keep you," he spluttered. "She said you were just a child. She made me say I'd give you back," he frowned. "But you're not a child anymore Jess," he smiled.

Give me back? Did he really say that? A glimmer of hope flickered through my mind, the faces of my parents smiling welcoming me home with open arms. Could it be true, would he let me go home?

"But," he said, eyes glaring down at me, "now that you've killed her. I don't have to give you back." He laughed a little, bent down, sniffed my hair and whispered deep into my ear, "you'll be mine forever now Jess, and we can look after our new children together... now hold still," he said, clambering behind himself, showing me the carving knife.

What was that for? My body tensed further, fists balled up and I squirmed under his weight. "Hold still damn you," he said as he leaned forward with the knife.

"No," I yelled. I couldn't cope with the thought of the pain he was about to inflict.

"What?" he asked, stunned at my insolence.

"No," I said, raising up my hands and grabbing his fist.

"But you aren't finished Jess," he said looking puzzled. "Your eyes are all wrong."

I gasped, he wanted to cut out my eyes. No! He can't! I won't let him! I lifted my pelvis, toppled him to the side, managed to free one of my legs and kicked him square in the chest. He fell backward. "No!" I yelled, screaming at the top of my lungs. Raising my foot, I kicked him again. His body bounded against the wall, knocking the crates flying. The candles toppled over, as fire warmed the room, teasing my skin with the lashings of burning guilt. Guilt that reigned through me. Guilt that I hadn't done something sooner, that I hadn't stood up, stopped him, become Gretel and saved her.

How dare he treat any of us like this? He's not God, he's far from the saviour he pretends he is. Keeping us locked up in a cage, pissing in buckets. I'm young, but I know one thing for sure, I'd be better dead than spend another minute trapped in here with this psycho.

He launched forward, anger filled his eyes like a madman on steroids. Fear gripped my backbone, held me down, frozen to the spot. He was coming, this was it, the end I'd wished for. Damn him, he'd win, and I'd have nothing left to lose. I lay there as he jumped on top of me, my neck gripped by his tortured expression. His fingers squeezed one by one. This was the end, I knew it, I felt it. And as my eyes dwindled I searched the room for her skinned head to say goodbye. She looked at me, her mouth opened in a scream as a spider crawled out through her open gaze. Between me and her, an object came into light, a thick handled object with a shiny blade attached. It couldn't be? Could it? The knife he'd wanted me to carve the roast with, the knife he'd threatened to cut my eyes out with. My fingertips scraped at the floor, pleading with my arm to allow them a step nearer. My neck burned from the tightness of his grip, the vessels in my eyes began to burst. My purple face gasped for breath as my mouth remained open, trapped in a silent scream forever more.

His knee pushed down on my chest as he shifted to grip me tighter. But with the movement of his weight, I managed to reach the knife, hold it tight in my dirtied hand and drive it into the side of him. Impaling it into his overweight stomach, blood pooled out, rushing away from him. His grip gave way as he pulled back, grabbed at the open wound screaming. His face paled as shock collapsed over his body, he sauntered backward, pushed on the stab wound trying to keep his blood inside, watching pale-faced as it fled from his fingertips.

My vision was distorted, my eyes ached from the blood that streamed from their sockets. Dizziness took over as I sat upright, trying to concentrate on the scene before me. My mind shook with what had just happened. My throat pained by the tightness of his grip. It hurt to speak. Hurt to breathe, and as I held my neck I crawled away. Protecting my fallen body with the carving knife, I cradled my legs, cocooning my innocence as I sat there watching. I waited for a few minutes, listened to the sounds of his gurgling breath, remaining in the darkness of the shadows that suffocated the corner. But even as much as I hated him, as much as I loathed the air he breathed. I couldn't watch, couldn't see his pain. He'd killed my friend. He'd taken five years of my life, destroying me from the inside out. I was nothing now, no longer a friend, no longer his captive, caged and bound. I was no-one. I sighed. It hurt to breathe, but I sighed again deeper and stronger. The pain kept me alive. The hurt made me see. I wasn't just his no-one anymore, I was someone, I was me. There was one person I could be for the girls, one-person Beth had asked me to be, that was her protector, her Gretel, just as Jess had been for me.

I couldn't keep hiding anymore. I had to stand in the light, face the reality, finish him off and take his keys. The thought of it was easy, but even that made me shake. The reality of it was much harder, he was there, dying, yet still alive. Whereas I was here, hidden, out of reach. I could wait for his death, wait for his suffering to end. Then I'd take the keys, free the children. But I didn't have the time. The crates were ablaze with a ferocity I'd only ever seen through his eyes. They could reach him before he died, they could take away his keys and our freedom along with it. What if he didn't die? What if he survived the stab wound? Had I impaled him in the proper place? I couldn't take that chance... if he survived, we'd all be in trouble. There would be no keys, no freedom, no life outside these walls. It'd be binbags and chainsaws and I couldn't subject the children to that.

He was slumped against the wall; the fire was licking at the crates beside him. Smoke filled the room, destroying my sight further. I had to get up, move, take the keys and release the children. But I had one thing to finish before I left. It would be hard, I knew this. But none of us were safe if he lived.

I stumbled forward on my knees, gripped the knife tight. Crawled across the floor, wary of the flames around me. Soon it would be too late in here, soon the fire would take over, burning us all to ash and cinder. There wasn't much time. It was now or never. I rose to my feet, fumbled my way forward, never taking my eyes from his cold expression. His dark brown eyes pierced through me, he glared as his body spasmed, and as I reached him, he was spitting blood, cursing the ground I walked on.

I kept my distance, sat beside him, out of reach. He glared at me, his cold eyes haunted by the screams of his past. I felt pity, my gut wrenched. Tears welled in my eyes, no person should die down here. But he had to. There was no choice in the matter. His death meant the beginning for all of us. I moved closer, the weapon gripped tighter in my shaky hand. "You deserve this," I said, kneeling beside him.

"Help me Jess," he asked, reaching out with a bloodied hand.

"No," I cried, tears falling from my eyes. I couldn't let him die thinking I was her. He had to remember. He needed to see. I pulled the knife upwards, felt for each knotted strand and cut away the mask he'd sewn onto me. I had released myself from his oppression, freed her face from my own. And as he saw me, the real me, he saw the tears I wept for his soul, the sorrow I felt for my fallen sister. I blinked, breathed in, raised the knife above my head and drove it down into his chest, impaling his ribcage as I stabbed him directly in the heart. The last face he saw before he died was mine, the real me. Mine was the face he'd take to his grave as he gasped, releasing his final breath. His eyes greyed over, his body slumped further. He was dead. His body limp and lifeless. He was gone. We were free.

Taking in a painful deep breath I sighed, released myself from the horror. I took his keys and left his psychotic body to the flames of savagery. The fire leaped at his legs, seethed through his clothing and boiled his skin down to the bone. I watched as he disappeared before my eyes. His carcass burned, it was the sweetest aroma I'd ever smelt, the scent of victory and the release of our punishment.

Hell had taken him. He was gone, but I was shocked it was so. I left the room, dizzy at the thought of freedom. My body torn down, battered and bruised. I limped through the tunnel, feeling across the wall to help keep my balance.

My fallen figure was in a state of shock, adrenaline fled as I succumbed to the agony I was truly in. I was afraid of every twist, every turn, worried he'd appear around the corner. Hallucinations made the shadows dance in delight. Swirling and twirling to the words "I'm free, I'm free." I wasn't sure what was real or what was not, as I fell to the floor.

Breathing in the smoke as it bellowed through the tunnel like a shroud of death and darkness. But through the darkness, I heard her, the mutterings through the walls, her wail of screams diminished. Jess was free, she was right by my side, taking my hand and guiding the way. I crawled forward, pushed along by her presence, reaching a light through the smoke, hearing the hum of the generator.

I found myself crawling into the room that held our cage. Three young faces looked up in horror, coughing and choking through their smoke-filled cage. Jess pulled me forward, as I threw Leah the keys then collapsed in a puddle on the ground. Leah fumbled, trying key after key as the fire raged, angry and needing to seethe the skin from its next victims. The sound of the cage opening echoed through the abandoned tunnels, splintering the barrier between fact and fiction. Jess was gone, reality hit hard. The girls were released. Tears flooded the room as they ran over, lifted me up and helped me walk. Susie cried, took my hand and pulled me up the metal stairs. Leah stayed behind me pushing me up, and all four of us rose into the sunshine, climbing our way to freedom, to our families and our lives once again.

5

Daylight bleached our eyes as each of us wandered blindly along the deserted road, reaching a highway, tired and in pain. We sat at the side in hope of rescue. Beth smiled, her cold ashen face warmed by the sunrise that soothed her tears. She sat beside me, comforting my cries as I held her tight. She leaned up, brushed my scraggly hair from my ears and whispered, "thank you, Gretel." She smiled, kissed my cheek, then stood up and joined Leah and Susie to flag down a car.

A beige Ford Escort pulled over with a dent on the back door, rusted wheel arches and chipped paint work. The drivers window wound down and an elderly lady peered out, staring over at us. "Do you need help?" she asked with a wary tone. Leah appeared to be talking to her, and Beth opened the back door, jumping in. My body ached as Susie helped me up. Broken ribs pierced my skin as I hobbled towards the vehicle, with a snail-like pace.

The lady stepped out in a knee length floral dress, a woollen cardigan, thick tights and comfortable shoes. "Oh, you poor girls, you do look a mess, here let me help you," she urged, taking my hand into hers; her red nail polish gleaming through the rays of the morning sun. She guided me over to the car, and I noticed her beautiful rose brooch on the side of her cardigan when she helped me in. Susie slid in after me, and Leah ran around to the front. The old lady closed the doors, sat in the driver's seat, and started the engine. As I fastened my seat belt I sat back, my muscles relaxing one by one. Sighing with relief I closed my eyes. My head pounded, and the pain of the last five years began to take its toll. Everything hurt, my body was battered and bruised, and no matter how hard I shut my eyes the image of his burning body, his piercing brown eyes wouldn't disappear.

Tears welled up, streaming down my bloody cheeks as I panted back a heart wrenching sob. "What happened?" the lady asked, as I sensed the concern in her tone. Leah spoke up. I continued to cry. She told the tale of a psychotic man, a scarred face with piercing brown eyes. She described our capture, our lives in the cage. Then her tears fell when she explained our escape through the fire, alluding at his final moments. The lady listened as she drove up a long, winding road, quietly taking in every word. She didn't say anything until Leah had finished. Then she coughed, choking back a cry, her knuckles white as she gripped at the steering wheel. Her actions spoke louder than words. She slammed on the brakes, turned the car around. I sat upright, wiped my tears and watched her anger form. Leah voiced concern as the lady grimaced at her, gritting her teeth.

"Where are we going?" Leah asked, her voice pitched with angst. The lady didn't respond. Her shoulders tensed, her teeth clenched. She looked in the rear-view mirror as her piercing brown eyes glared at me. Familiarity struck a nerve, something was wrong with this picture.

I gripped Susie's hand, "what?" she asked, her brow furrowed, eyes narrow.

"She…" I said, unsure of how to finish the sentence. My chest tightened as I panicked, body tense, mouth open.

"What?" Beth asked, taking my hand, staring into my wide eyes.

The car sped back down the road, engine roaring, Leah began to scream, gripping the dashboard. Beth woke, grabbed my arm as Susie began to pull at the door handle. I reached forward, clasping the cold plastic, pulling and pulling but it wouldn't budge. The doors were locked, closing us off from the outside world. I turned to see Beth's face drain of all colour, her eyes wide, mouth open as she screamed.

"Where are you taking us?" I yelled. Body tense, fists balled. She pushed down on the accelerator again, speeding up as the deserted landscape hurtled by.

"Stop the car!" I yelled, "Stop it now!" I leaned forward, gripping my ribs as an immense pain shot through me. Grabbing her shoulder, I tried to reach to get to the central locking button. She slapped my hand away with such force, that it stung, swerving the car, knocking me sideways.

"You'll pay for what you did to my son," she scolded.

My mind froze, mouth agape. I sat back defeated, my face as white as snow.

The rear-view mirror reflected the lady's wild brown eyes, she scowled, speeding up.

"Don't worry girls, Mama will take care of you."

GRETEL

AUTHOR'S NOTE

Thank you for reading Gretel. I hope you enjoyed the story! I always appreciate your feedback and would really be grateful it if you could leave me a review on Amazon or Goodreads – just a few words like "I liked it" is great. It makes all the difference!

As with all new authors, reviews mean the world to me. It keeps me going, helps me strengthen my writing style and help's this story become a success. If you enjoyed reading Gretel and like to read thrillers with a supernatural side to them, then my four-book series would be right up your street. The first book can be found on Amazon and is called Eternal Entity, part of The Celestial Rose series.

ANNALEE ADAMS

ETERNAL ENTITY

BOOK ONE
OF THE CELESTIAL ROSE SERIES

Connect with Annalee

Join Annalee on social media. She is regularly posting videos and updates for her next books on TikTok and Facebook.

Join Annalee in her Facebook group:

Annalee Adams Bookworms & Bibliophiles.

Also, subscribe to Annalees newsletter through her website - for free books, sales, sneak previews and much more.

Subscribe at www.AnnaleeAdams.biz

TikTok: @author_annaleeadams

Website: www.AnnaleeAdams.biz

Email: AuthorAnnaleeAdams@gmail.com

Facebook:
https://www.facebook.com/authorannaleeadams/

Other books by Annalee Adams

ABOUT THE AUTHOR

Annalee Adams was born in Ashby de la Zouch, England. Annalee spent much of her childhood engrossed in fictional stories. Starting with teenage point horror stories and moving on up to the works of Stephen King and Dean Koontz. However, her all-time favourite book is Lewis Carroll's, Alice in Wonderland.

Annalee lives in the UK with her supportive husband, two fantastic children, little dog, and kitten. She's a lover of long walks on the beach, strong cups of tea and reading a good book by candlelight.

Made in the USA
Monee, IL
09 August 2022